PUZZLE TRAIN

Susannah Leigh

Illustrated by Brenda Haw

Contents

Series Editor: Gaby Waters
Assistant Editor: Michelle Bates

About this book

This book is about a boy called Alex. Alex wants to drive trains when he grows up. There are puzzles to solve on every double page. If you get stuck, you can look at the answers on pages 31 and 32.

Alex

Puzzle Train

←Bert

Alex has a friend called Bert. This is Bert. He is the driver of Puzzle Train. Puzzle Train is a steam train.

Fred

Fred is the fireman on Puzzle Train. He is in charge of the fire that heats the water that makes the steam that makes Puzzle Train go.

One day, Alex gets a telephone call from Bert.

Hello Alex. I am driving Puzzle Train to the seaside on Saturday and I need some help. Would you like to come and blow the whistle for me?

Yes please!

2

Things to spot

On every double page, there is a piece of special train kit to collect. Can you find everything?

cap

coal shovel

belt

useful keys

jacket

tool kit

lunch box

watch

badge

coal bucket

fire protection gloves

train book

whistle

The Lightning Locomotive
The Lightning Locomotive is faster than Puzzle Train, but it is smokier and noisier. The two drivers, Jaz and Jez and their pet crow, Caw think the Lightning Locomotive should be the only train to go to the seaside. You won't see Jaz and Jez on every double page, but watch out for Caw!

Caw

Jaz

STOP!

Jez

Lost property
People are always losing things on train journeys. There is at least one lost red umbrella hiding on every double page. See if you can find them all.

At the station

Alex arrived at the station on Saturday morning. He was looking forward to his day out on Puzzle Train.

Alex looked around at the busy platform. He wondered who would be on Puzzle Train today. He listened carefully to what everyone was saying and soon he knew.

Can you guess which passengers are taking Puzzle Train today?

5

We're off!

Alex looked at the clock. It was time for Puzzle Train to go.

"All aboard!" Alex called. He made sure all the doors were closed and everyone was safely on. He waved his flag and blew his whistle. He hopped up to join Bert and Fred, and then Puzzle Train was off, chugging slowly out of the station.

They passed houses, schools ...

... and factories.

Soon they were steaming through the countryside.

Alex stood on the foot plate as Puzzle Train
chuffed along the tracks. Alex turned around
to see the trail of smoke billowing behind
them. Suddenly, through the smoke, he
spotted something very wrong indeed.

What has Alex seen?

SEASIDE

Tickets please!

Someone was trying to climb aboard Puzzle Train! Alex ran past the coal tender and through the train. But the open door was now closed, and there was no one in sight. How strange! But Alex couldn't worry about it now, because he had an important job to do. It was time to collect all the passengers' tickets.

TICKETS

children

grown ups

old folk

animals

IDENTITY CARDS

children 16

old folk 60

It wasn't an easy task. Almost everybody had the wrong tickets. Some children had grown-ups' tickets and some grown-ups had animals' tickets. There were all kinds of other mistakes.

Alex looked carefully at the ticket board.

Then he looked at everyone's tickets. Some people had identity cards as well. It was quite a muddle, but soon Alex had sorted everything out and he knew what to do.

Which passengers need new tickets?

Trouble on the tracks

Alex changed the last passenger's ticket. Then he walked back to the front of the train just as it was slowing down. A spotted cow was crossing the track ahead.

"Alex," said Bert. "To drive a train well, you must always be observant. Look around you and keep your eyes peeled all the time. Can you see any other obstacles on the tracks?"

Can you?

Trouble on the train

Toot! Toot! went the whistle on Puzzle Train. The spotted cow wandered away and they sped on. Suddenly there was a loud screeching noise and Puzzle Train stopped.

"Someone has pulled the emergency brake!" cried Bert. "They must be in trouble. We'll have to check the train and the tracks."

Alex ran through the train.

Fred ran down the track.

Pull in emergency

Bert ran up the track.

But no one was in trouble!

Alex arrived back at the cab at the same time as Bert and Fred. They hadn't seen anyone in trouble either. Then Alex gave a shout.

"What has happened to the fire, Fred?" he cried.

Do you know?

Lightning strikes!

Fred looked at the boiler and groaned.

"Someone has thrown water on this fire," he said. "It will take time to get it going again."

Just then, the Lightning Locomotive hurtled past, stirring up a howling wind as it went. Jaz and Jez grinned and waved.

TOOT!

"I'll bet that sneaky pair had something to do with this!" spluttered Bert through the thick smoke.

The Lightning Locomotive sped off and Alex saw that it had left a trail of trouble behind.

Can you see what has happened?

Tunnel maze

Soon they were ready to go again and Puzzle Train steamed after the Lightning Locomotive into a tunnel. A maze of tracks led out to several different places.

"We've got to find the way out to the seaside," said Bert. "But we'll have to be careful. There are some tricky track changes ahead."

Can you find the way out to the seaside?

TO PUZZLE TOWN

TO PUZZLE MOUNTAIN

TO PUZZLE PLANET

In the country

Puzzle Train chugged safely out of the dark tunnel and slowed to a stop at a little country station.

"All aboard for the seaside!" Alex called.

"We can't go yet!" cried the passengers. "The Lightning Locomotive sped through here so fast it blew away our seaside things. Can you help us find them all?"

Alex listened as the passengers told him what they had lost, and then he found everything.

Can you find all the lost seaside things?

19

Messy mail

When everything was found, Puzzle Train set off again. As Alex walked past the mail van, a shout from Mel, the very new mail girl, stopped him.

"Alex," she said, "I have to sort out all these letters. Some are for the seaside, and some aren't. But I'm new at this job and I don't think I can do it by myself. Can you help me?"

"Of course," said Alex. He put all the mail for the seaside into the right pigeon holes, and the rest of the mail into big baskets.

Can you sort out the mail?

Lunch time

Alex waved goodbye to Mel and walked through the train. When he came to the dining car, he found Billy the cook looking cross.

"Alex," he cried. "Wilma the waitress isn't here today, and I'm all confused with these passengers' orders. Can you help?"

Alex listened to all the orders and looked at the menu board. He soon saw the problem. Some people hadn't read the menu carefully and wanted food that they couldn't have.

Which people can't have everything they want?

I'll have fish, mushrooms and a cherryberry ice cream.

NO CHICKEN TODAY

Bill, I'm ill. Love Wil x

All clear!

Alex left nearly everyone munching happily on their food and made his way back to Bert's cab. Puzzle Train was slowing down as it reached a junction.

"We'll have to be careful here, Alex," said Bert. "We have to find a track that leads to the seaside and a signal which tells us it's all clear to go."

BLUE TRAINS ONLY

SEASIDE

PUZZLE TRAIN SIGNALS

STOP!

DON'T GO!

WAIT!

ALL CLEAR!

WARNING! – GO SLOWLY

GO CAREFULLY!

24

SEASIDE

SEASIDE

PUZZLE
PARK

SEASIDE

Alex looked at his signal guide and at the tracks
in front of him. He soon found a track which led to
the seaside and was clear to go along.

Which track should they go along?

Crash!

They steamed on to the sea but they didn't get very far. Just ahead, the Lightning Locomotive had come off the tracks! Its passengers stood next to it.

"What happened here?" Alex asked.

Everybody began to talk at once, but what they said was all muddled. Alex listened carefully. Soon he had put everyone's stories in the right order.

Look at all the little pictures opposite. Can you put them in order and tell the story of what happened to the Lightning Locomotive?

SEASIDE

THIS WAY

The seaside at last

"Climb aboard," said Bert to the Lightning Locomotive's passengers. "We'll take you to the seaside."

Everyone was very glad to be rescued. At last they arrived at the seaside. They all had a great afternoon.

"I wonder what happened to Jaz and Jez?" said Alex.

"Never mind them," said Fred, slurping his ice cream. "Let's go for a swim!"

Can you see what has happened to Jaz and Jez?

SEASIDE

29

Time to go home

All too soon it was time to go back. It had been a wonderful afternoon. Everyone climbed aboard Puzzle Train and they set off for home. Even Jaz and Jez hitched a lift.

As Puzzle Train chuffed slowly through the countryside, Jaz and Jez looked down from Bert's cab and gasped in amazement.

"What lovely scenery!" they said. "The Lightning Locomotive went too fast for us to notice anything."

"So you didn't spot the blue rabbits on the way?" asked Alex.

Did you? There is one on almost every double page, and on this one too!

Answers

Pages 4-5
At the station

The passengers who are taking Puzzle Train today are circled in black.

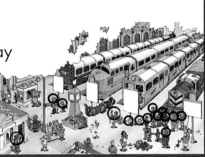

Pages 6-7
We're off!

Alex has seen someone jumping onto Puzzle Train. Their foot is circled here. (Could it be that sneaky Jez?)

Pages 8-9
Tickets please!

The passengers who need new tickets are circled in black.

Pages 10-11
Trouble on the tracks

The obstacles on the tracks are circled in black.

Pages 12-13
Trouble on the train

The fire that was blazing in the boiler has been put out with water. (Could Jez have done it?)

Pages 14-15
Lightning strikes!

The black circles show the trouble the Lightning Locomotive has caused.

Pages 16-17
Tunnel maze

The way out to the seaside is marked in black.

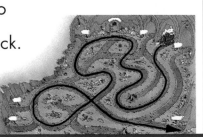

Pages 18-19
In the country

The lost seaside things are circled in black.

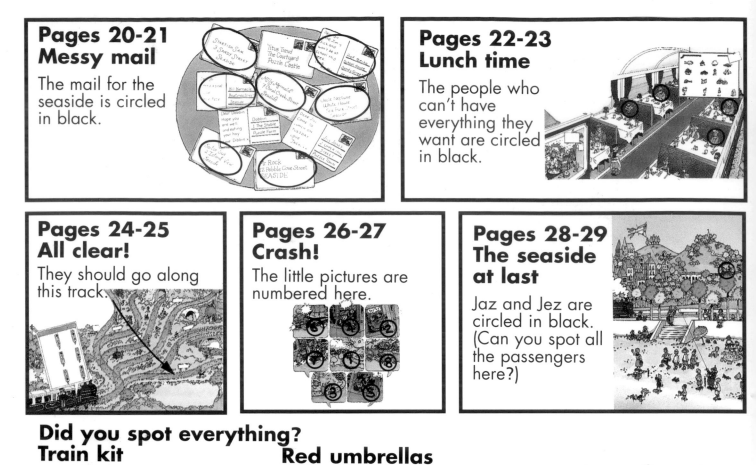

Pages 20-21
Messy mail

The mail for the seaside is circled in black.

Pages 22-23
Lunch time

The people who can't have everything they want are circled in black.

Pages 24-25
All clear!

They should go along this track.

Pages 26-27
Crash!

The little pictures are numbered here.

Pages 28-29
The seaside at last

Jaz and Jez are circled in black. (Can you spot all the passengers here?)

Did you spot everything?
Train kit
Red umbrellas

Did you remember to spot a piece of special kit on each double page? Did you find all the lost red umbrellas?

Jaz and Jez and Caw the crow

Did you see Caw the crow lurking on every double page? He was acting as a lookout for Jaz and Jez. Sometimes you may have spotted that sneaky pair too.

Pages	Train kit	Red umbrellas
4-5	cap	two
6-7	jacket	one
8-9	useful keys	three
10-11	tool kit	three
12-13	watch	two
14-15	coal shovel	one
16-17	belt	three
18-19	badge	two
20-21	whistle	three
22-23	train book	one
24-25	coal bucket	three
26-27	gloves	two
28-29	lunch box	three

This edition first published in 2003 by Usborne Publishing Ltd., Usborne House, 83-85 Saffron Hill, London EC1N 8RT, England.

www.usborne.com Copyright © 2003, 1995
Usborne Publishing Ltd.

First published in America August 1995.